STEAL THEIR STYLE!

Meet the models and check out their outfits! Then use their looks and style tips to inspire the designs for your own fashion show later in the book.

For a great party outfit, try a knee-length asymmetric dress. The pleats on this one create stunning curves that offset the single shoulder. Stick to one colour for high impact!

Maisy has nailed the perfect daytime look! Her pretty maxi dress is toughened up with a leather jacket. Orange stitching that picks out her hair colour ties the outfit together.

PRETTY AND GIRLIE

Every girl likes to look pretty. Flower prints and floaty dresses are really fun to design and remember that pastel colours are key to defining this delicate look. Don't be afraid to accessorise, but keep it subtle and let the clothes do the talking.

Lauren
LIKES: Painting her nails
DISLIKES: Washing up dishes
FASHION STYLE: Elegant

Anna
LIKES: High heels
DISLIKES: Snakes
FASHION STYLE: Confident mix

This delicate butterfly print cardigan teamed with pastel green trousers creates a gorgeous daytime outfit. Shoes, lips and nails in dusky pink complete the look.

Ruffles, lace and soft pastel shades combine in this super-cute outfit! Anna's top has a curved Peter Pan collar, which echoes the scalloped layers on her skirt.

MODERN DENIM

Sam
LIKES:
Pop concerts
DISLIKES:
Tying her hair up
FASHION STYLE:
Casual

Mia
LIKES:
Her curly hair
DISLIKES:
Rain!
FASHION STYLE:
Funky

Denim doesn't have to be blue. Coloured jeans are a trend that is here to stay. A key styling tip is to pair them with a neutral colour so they really pop!

A tailored dress is a great way to wear denim. Military-style buttons and puff sleeves make this one seriously stylish. Brass-buckled ankle boots complete the outfit.

Denim will always be in fashion! But it doesn't mean you have to stick to those plain blue jeans. Modern denim is all about different shapes and colours. Try bright, ice-cream coloured jeans, or a tailored dress for a new twist on this classic fabric.

BOLD AND BRIGHT

You'll stand out from the crowd in these bright eye-catching outfits! Use the rainbow as your inspiration to look bold and vibrant whatever the occasion. Start by choosing one bright colour, and as your confidence grows, add more!

Bright, bold panels of colour, broken by solid black lines are not only eye-catching but also a huge fashion statement. Black heels with cut-outs echo the panels in the dress.

Try different colour combinations to test out what's hot and what's not! This outfit combines four bright, block colours perfectly!

ANIMAL PRINT

Follow these style tips to ensure you use animal prints to their best advantage. Take a walk on the wild side with leopard, tiger and snake prints and let your designs be as fierce as your inspiration! This is a great trend to try a little, or a lot of!

Mix and match prints with solid colours. The neutral tones in this snake print dress are complemented by Lauren's hot pink jacket and shoes.

Strong, animal print accessories can give even the most basic of outfits a high-fashion edge. Here, the leopard print makes Maisy's tame outfit roar!

VINTAGE CHIC

This flirtatious 1950s style dress with its super-cute shape is simply irresistible! Pair with matching red shoes, a big bow and bright lips and you're ready to go.

Nothing screams all-American high school cool louder than a classic letterman jacket! Aki looks perfectly preppy in his, paired with a casual shirt and chinos.

Fashion is always cutting-edge, but that doesn't mean you can't wear styles from the past. You can add on-trend accessories to give them a modern twist. These outfits are inspired by stylish looks from the past, and can still be seen on catwalks today!

Boho-chic is still big news! A floaty, patterned dress accessorised with a wide-brimmed hat and plenty of beads, gives this 1960s look a 'hippy chick' vibe.

Flapper dresses don't have to be trapped in the 1920s. This luscious silk dress, with a mesh trim, drop waist and graphic print looks just as fresh on today's catwalks.

METALLICS

A gold jacket instantly adds an edgy glamour to an everyday outfit. Add a matching clutch bag with sequin detail to turn an understated outfit into an eye-catching fashion hit.

Lauren's futuristic look pairs multicoloured metallic stripes with a single-colour skirt in a contrasting texture. Pick out a colour in the top for your shoes to pull the outfit together.

This can be a tricky trend to pull off, but if it's done well, it will inject a glitzy dose of glamour into your wardrobe! Be sure to pick eye-friendly tones that compliment your model's natural colouring, so she'll shimmer and shine in the spotlight!

This outfit sings, 'elegance'! You can't get more glam than a slinky gold maxi! To make your fabric look like molten metal, use soft, wavy vertical lines in the shading and add bright white highlights.

This body-con beauty looks great on Holly! Use lots of highlights to achieve this shimmering effect when colouring your own metallic fabrics.

RED CARPET

The red carpet is the home of glamour. This beautifully fitted fishtail dress, in a colour that demands attention, will make your model look like a Hollywood star at any event.

Upgrade a classic suit by going for a strong, eye-catching pattern like plaid. Keep the tie subtle though. Less is sometimes more when it comes to accessories – let the suit do the talking!

Check out our models, working the red carpet! When the eyes of the world are upon you, it's all about making a statement. Use striking silhouettes, luxurious fabrics and a good helping of classic glamour to give your star outfit maximum impact!

A stunning, sequinned dress will shimmer in the flashing lights of camera bulbs. Simple, toned down accessories help make the dress, and the model, the main attraction.

The little black dress will never go out of fashion! Try giving it a twist by adding soft, textured fabrics, sheer lace, or both! Accessorise with bright red lips!

START DESIGNING!

Time to create your own collection! Start by pencilling in the shape of your clothing over the figure outline. Add pattern and colour, then the show can begin!

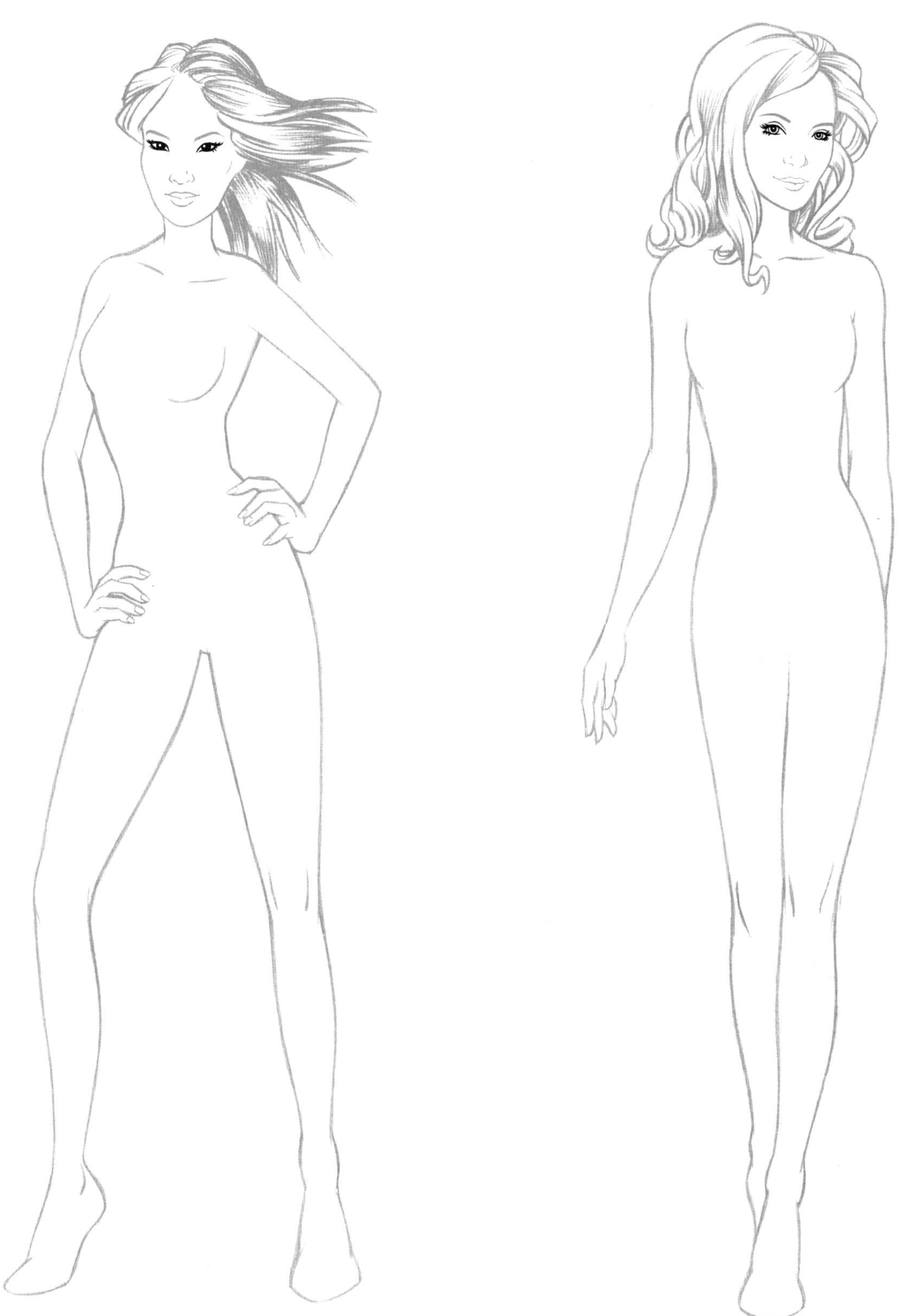

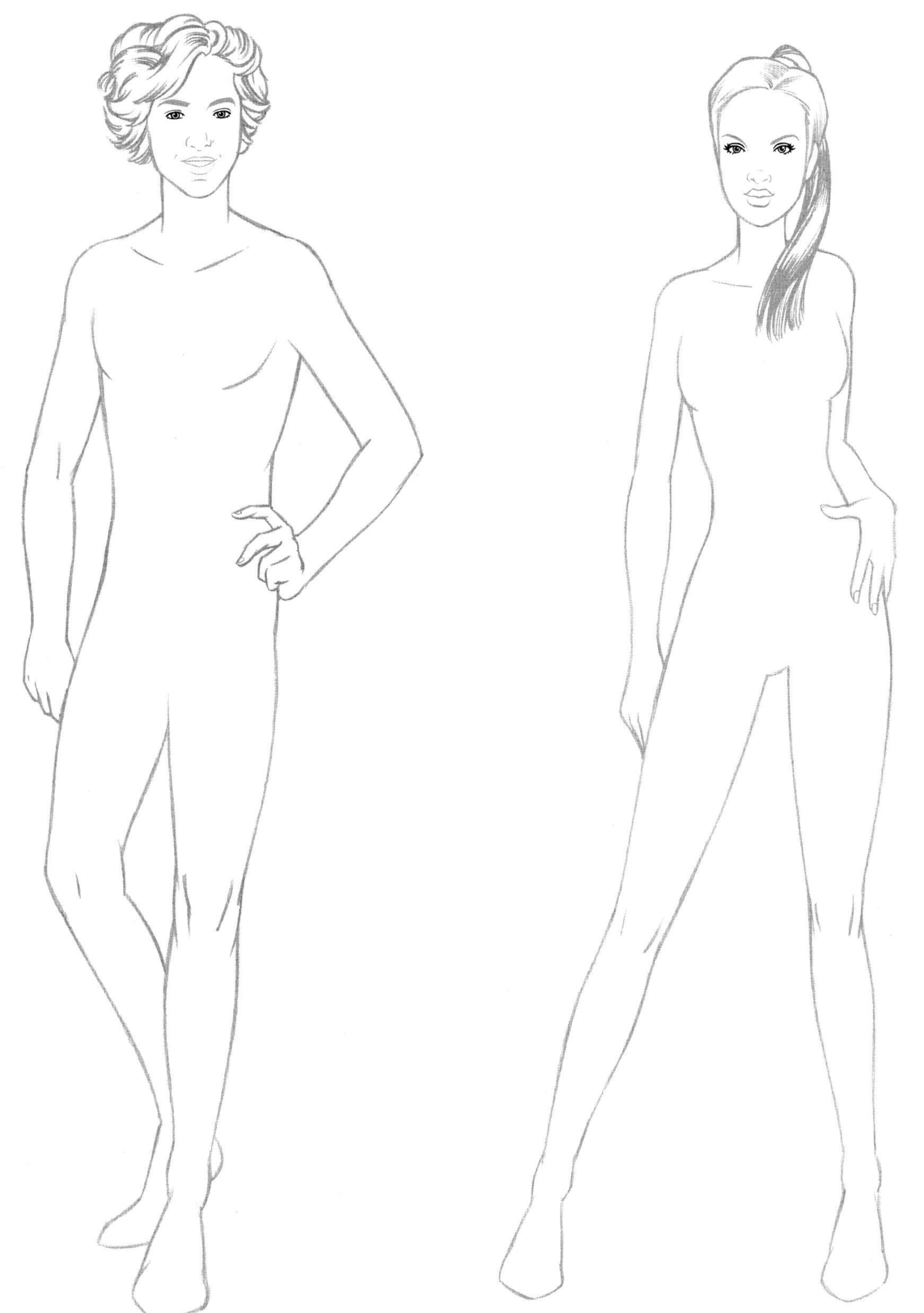

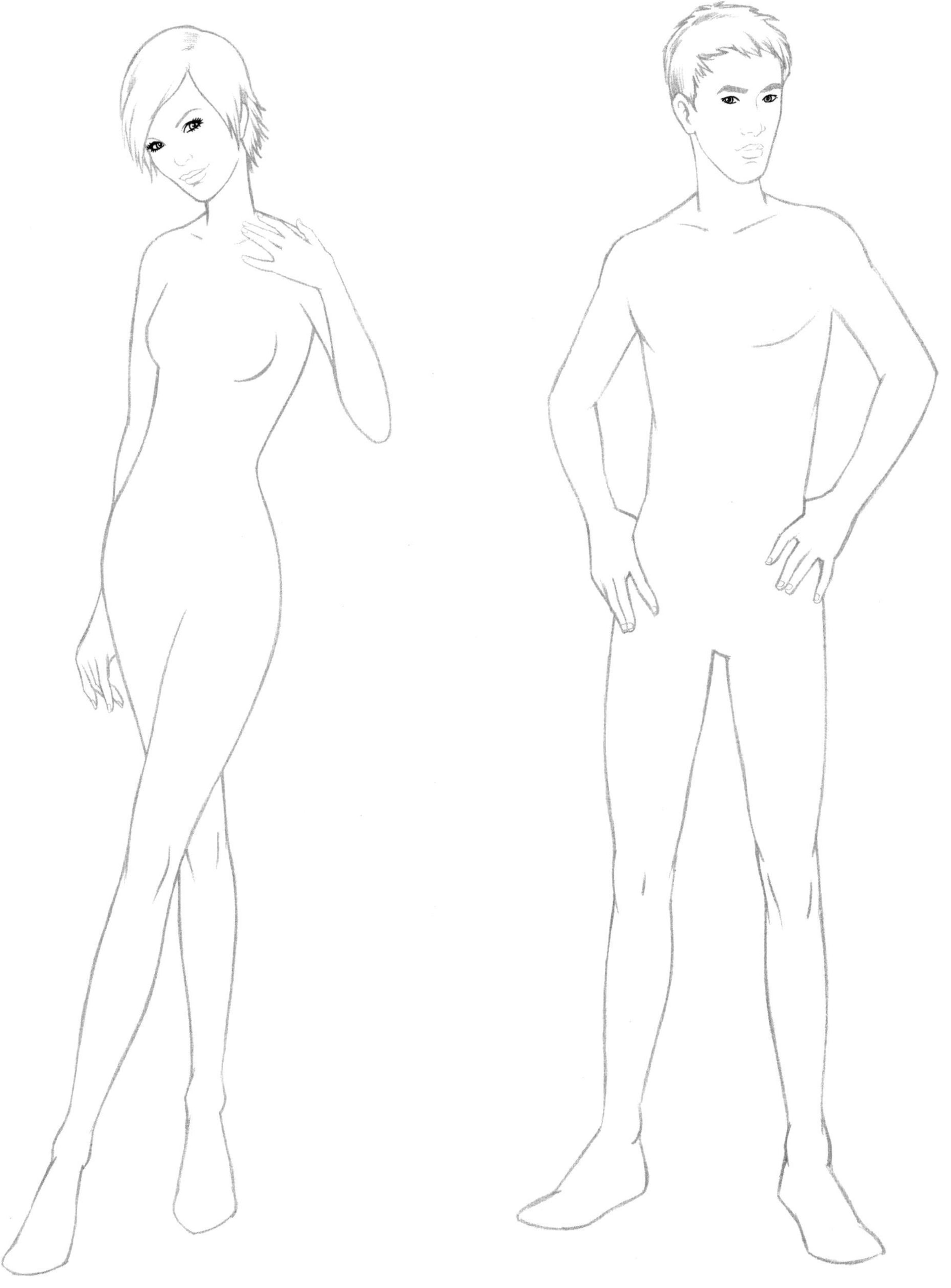

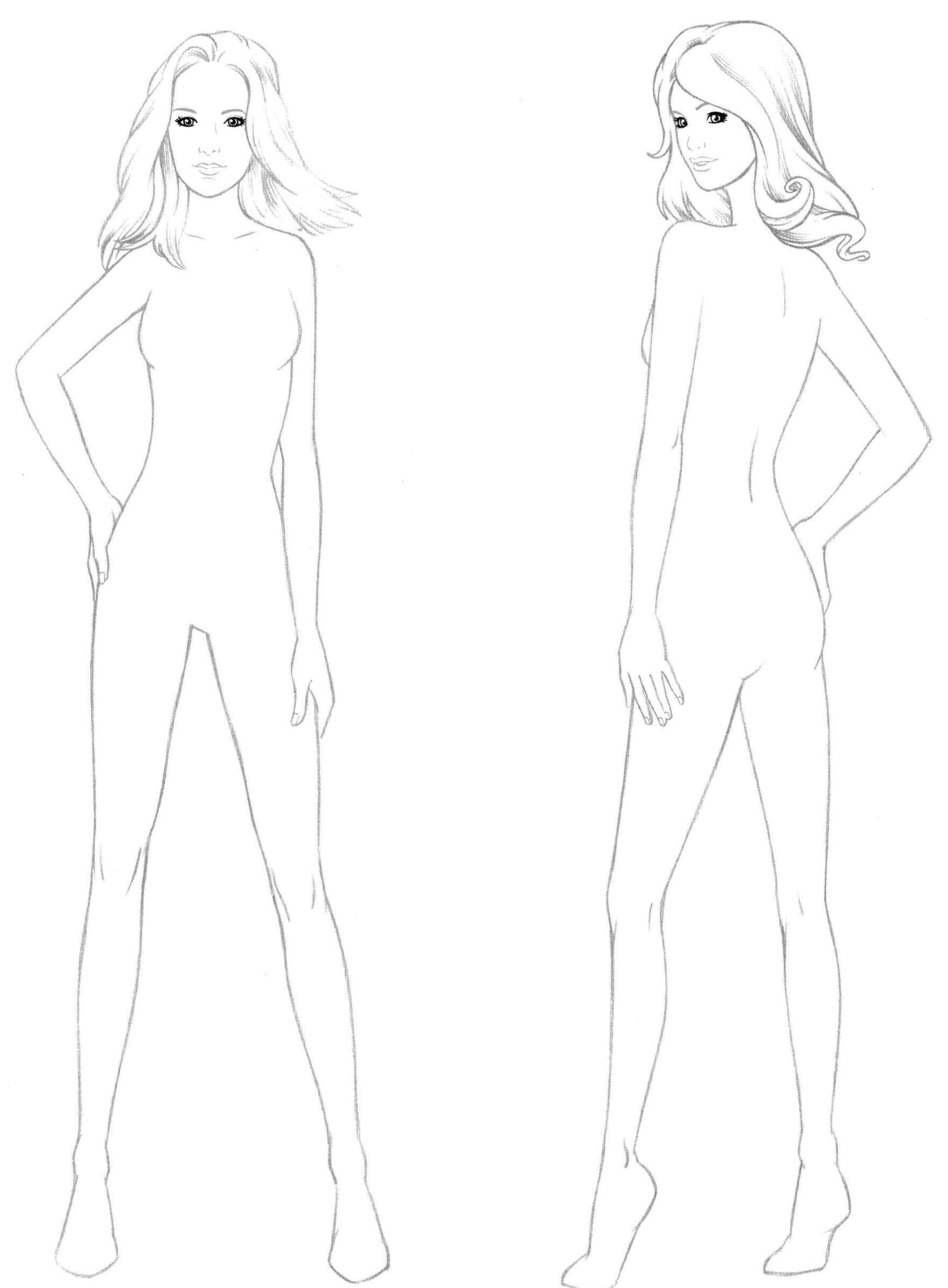

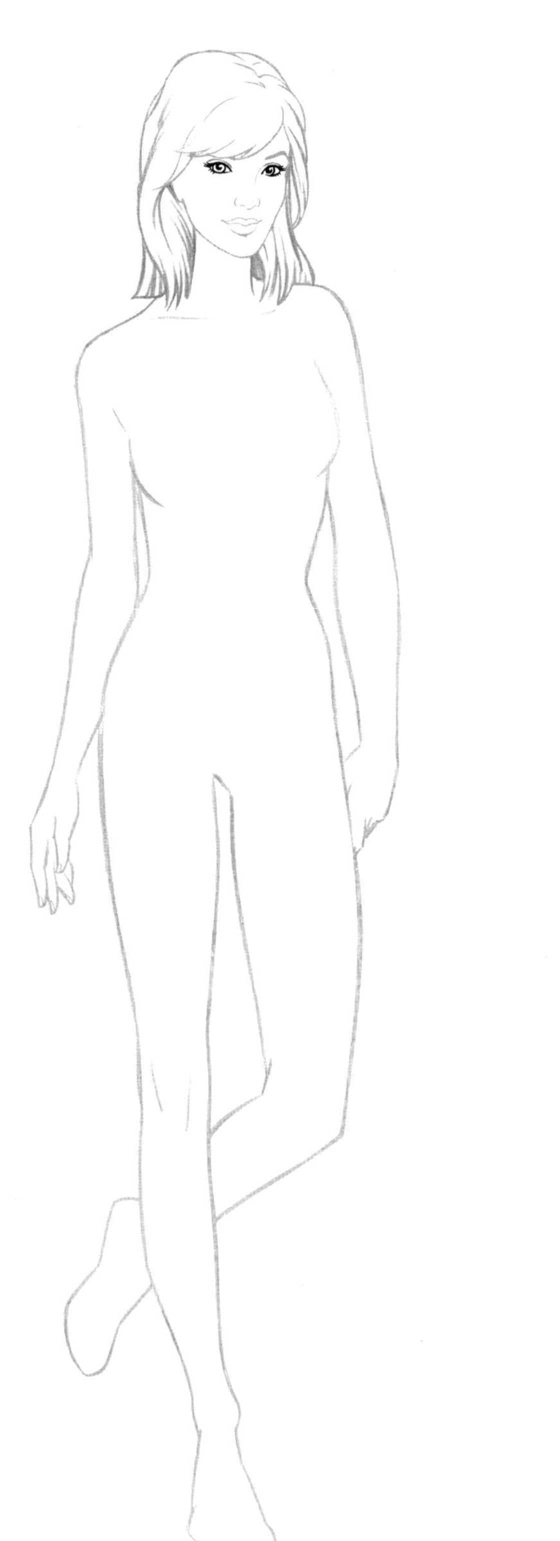

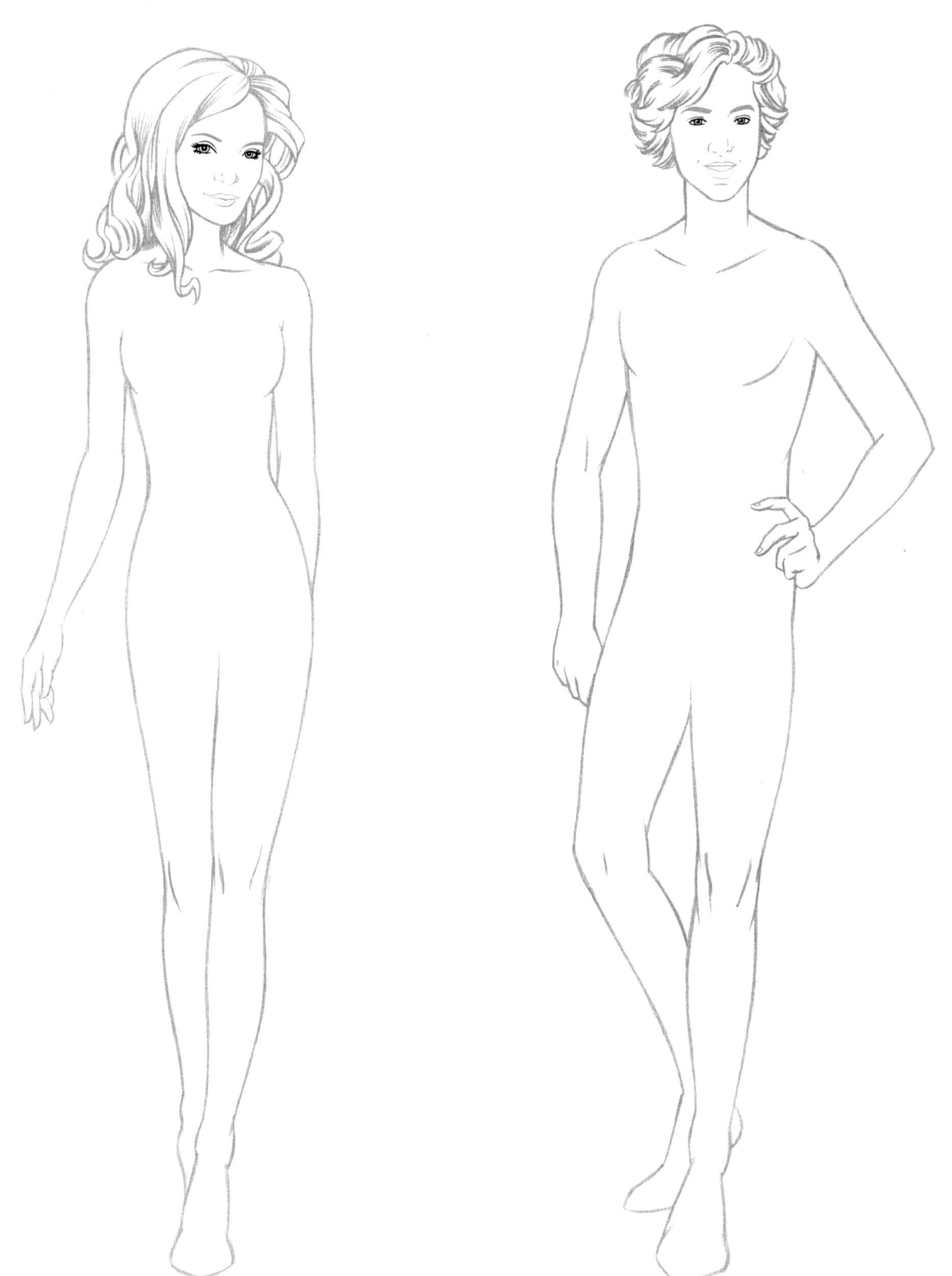

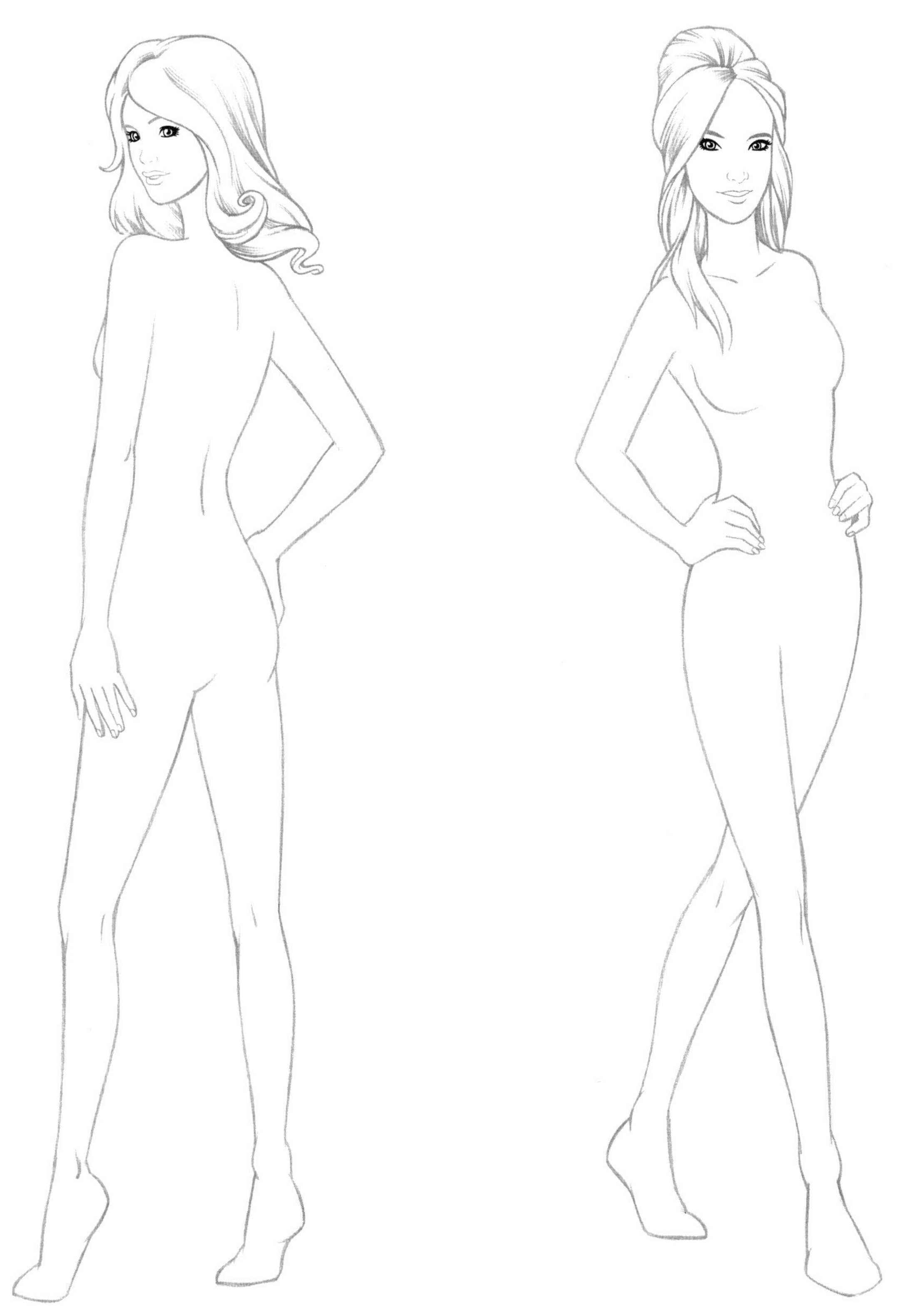

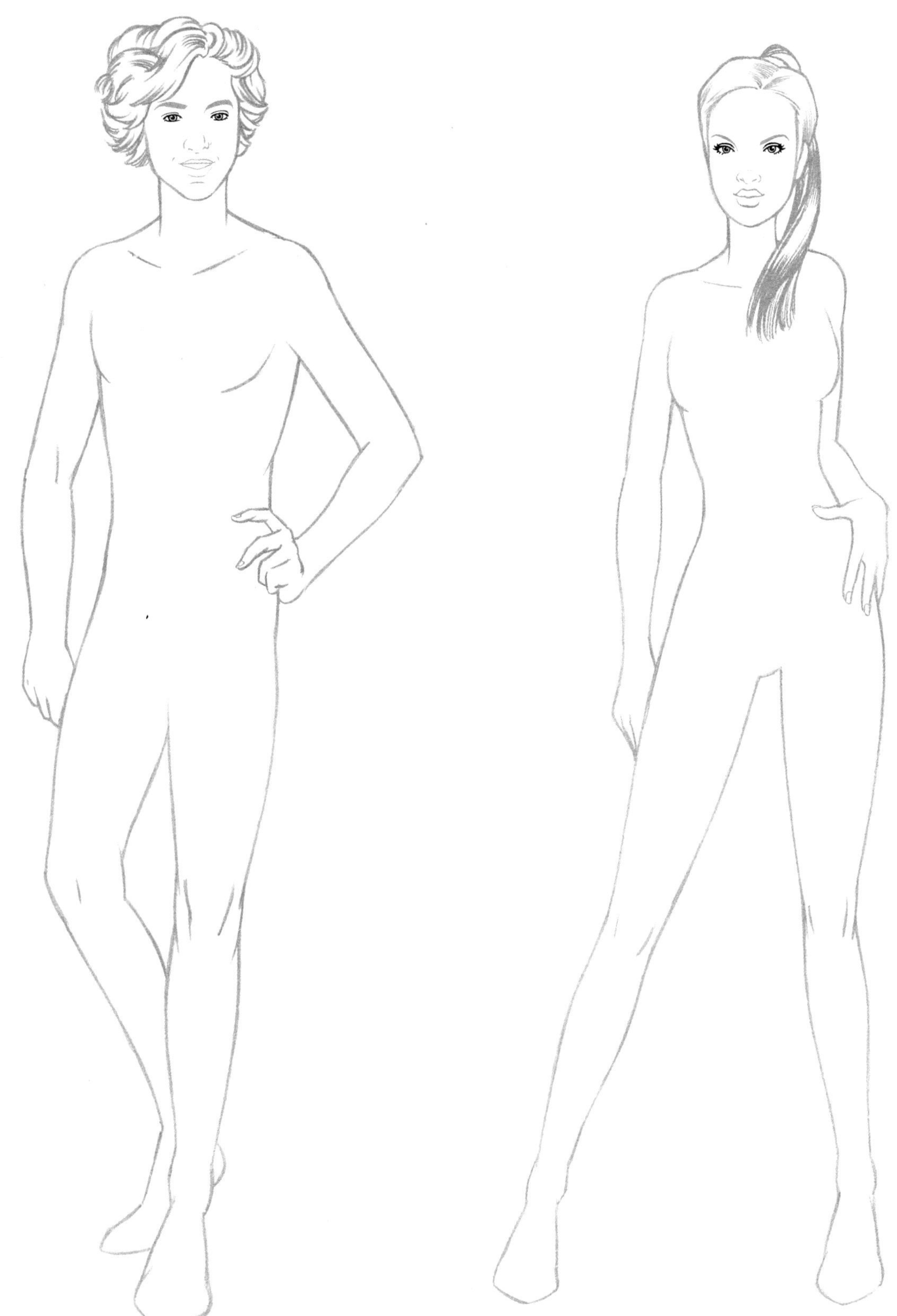

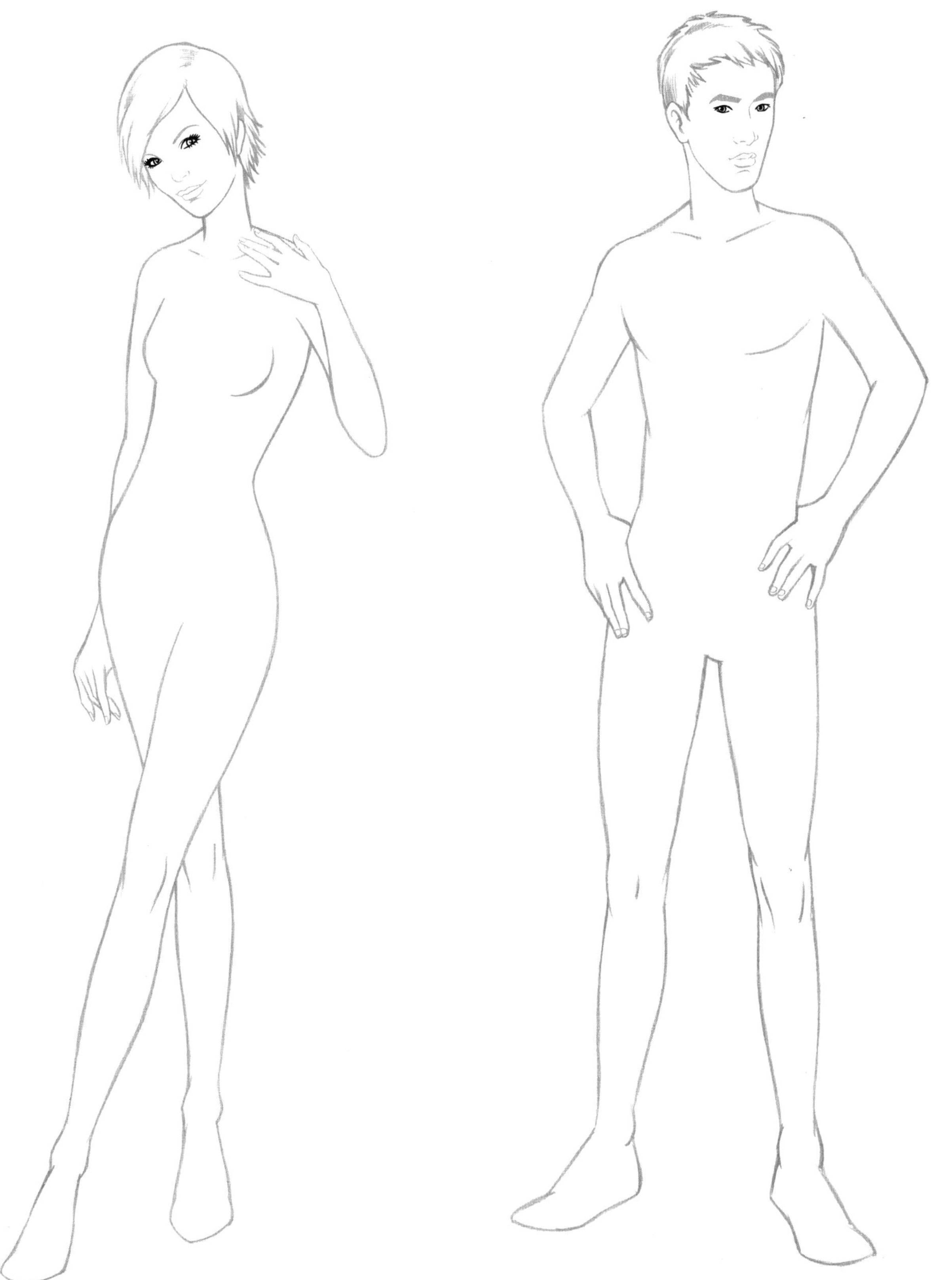

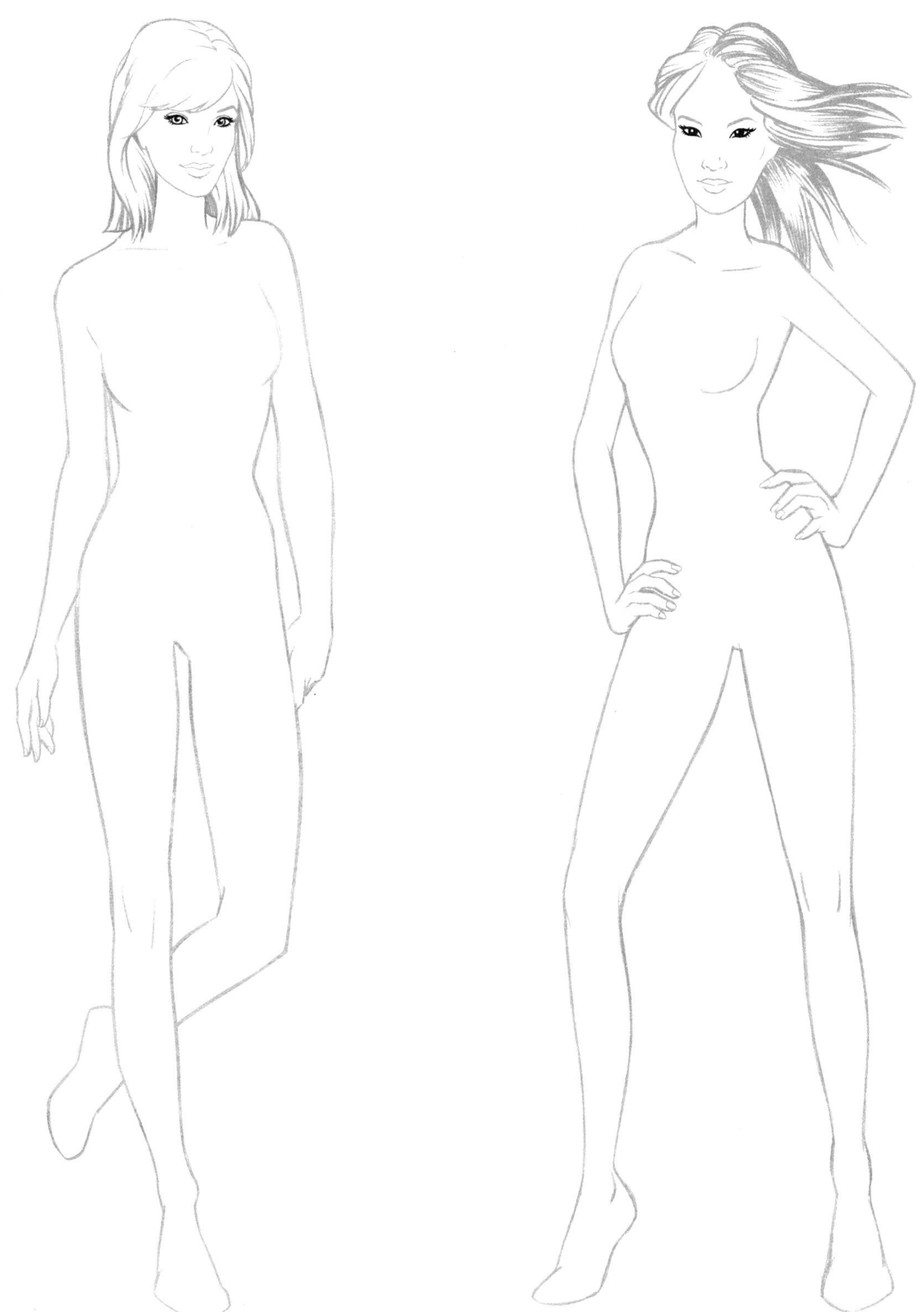

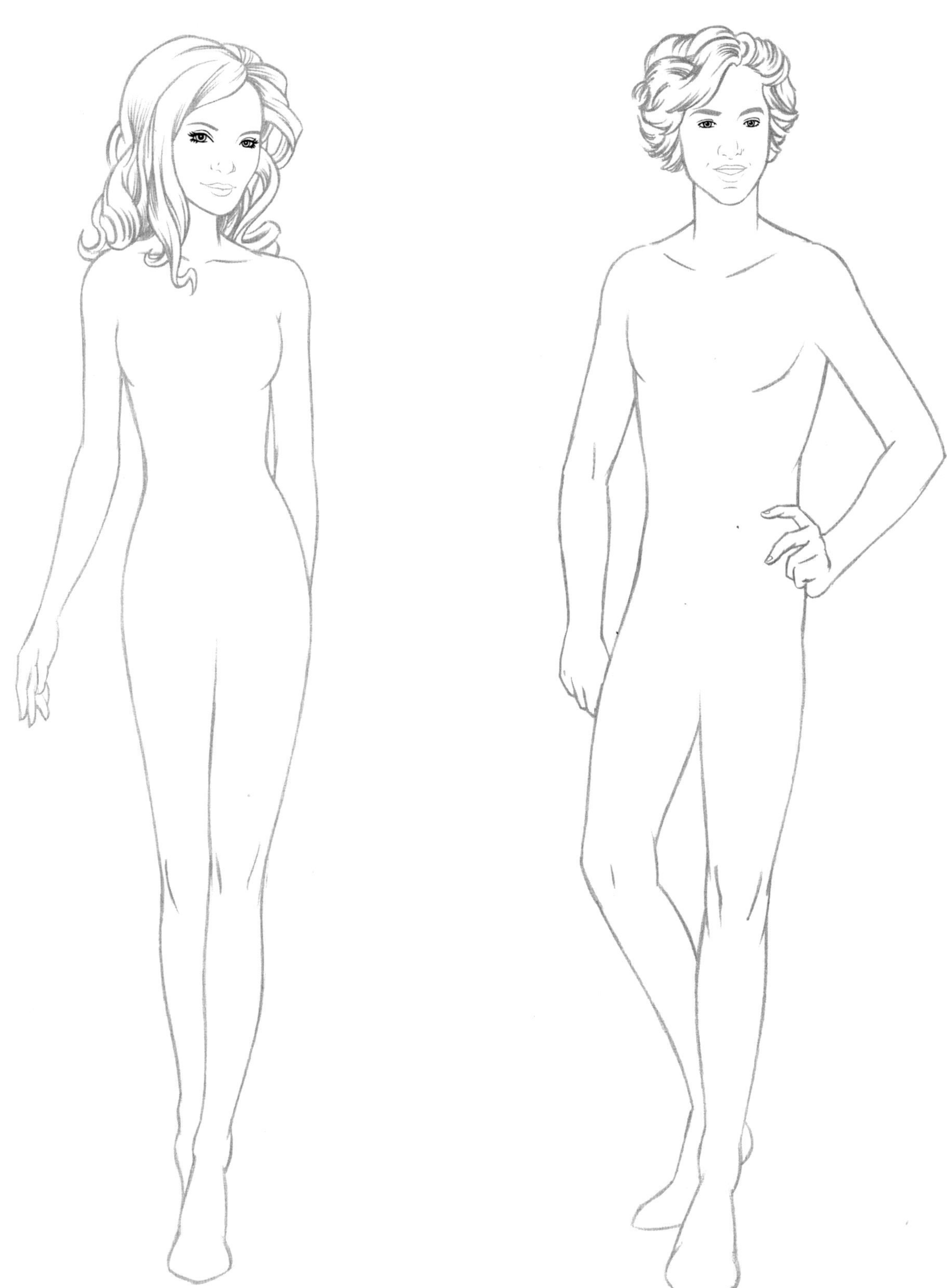

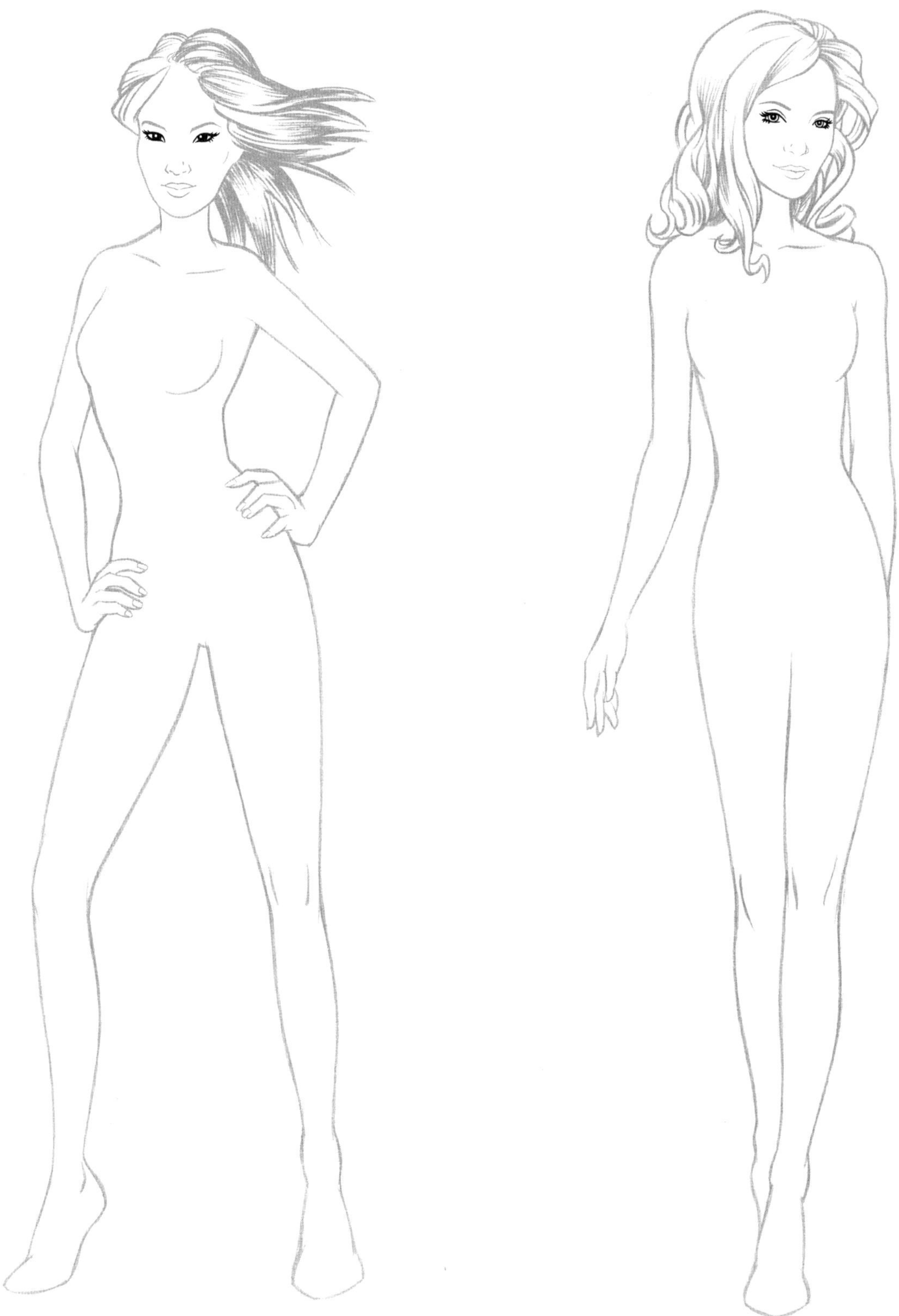

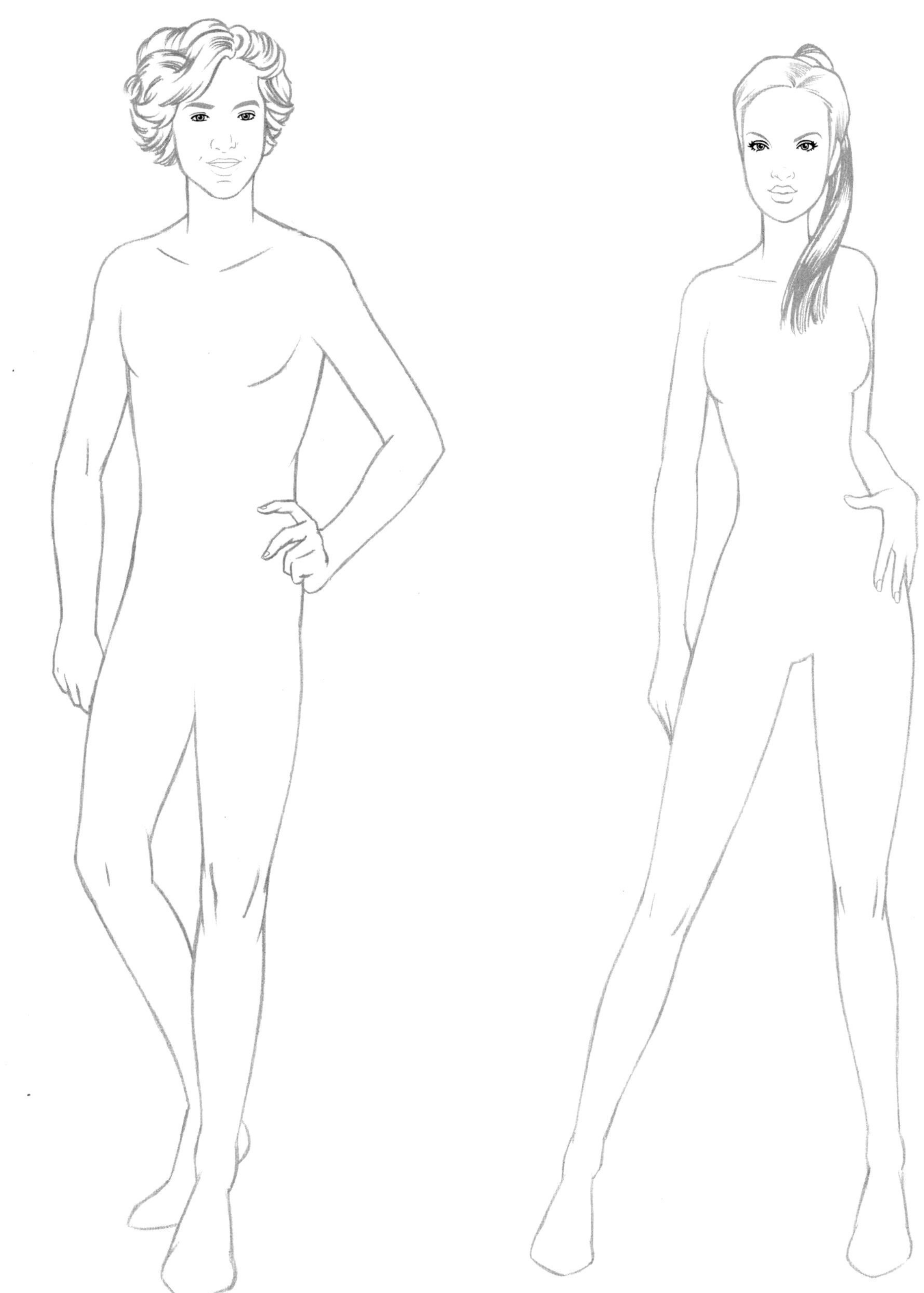

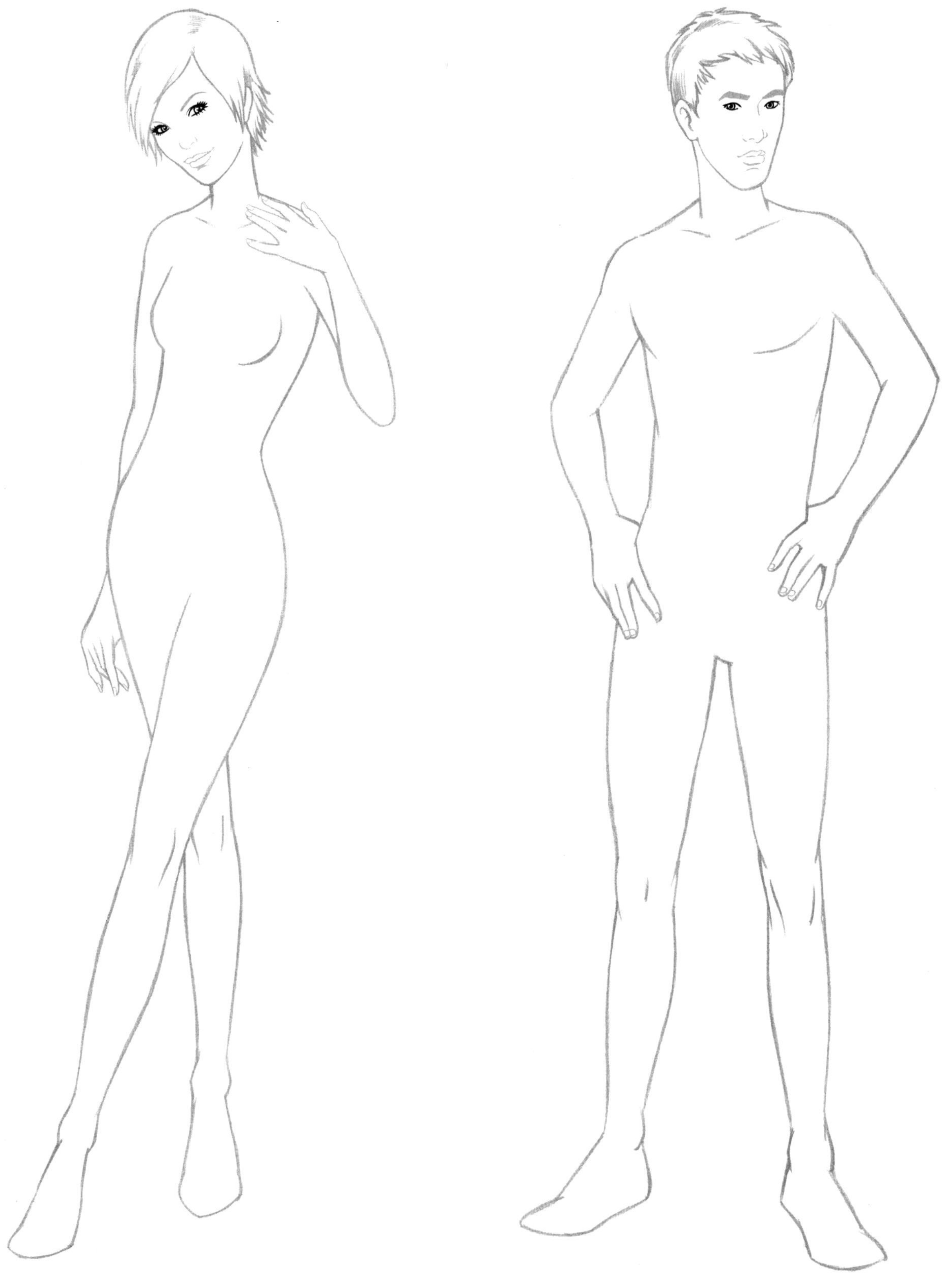

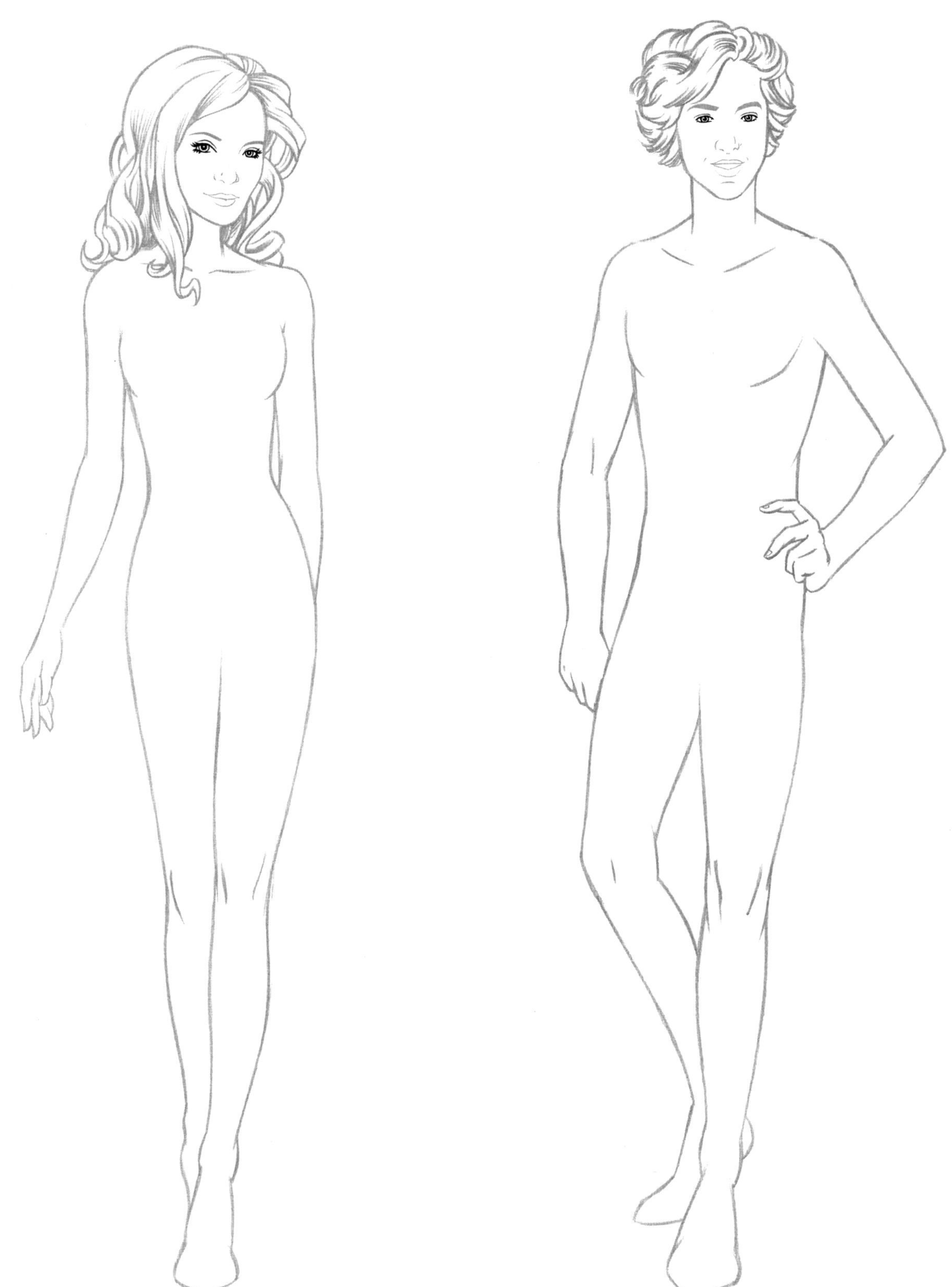

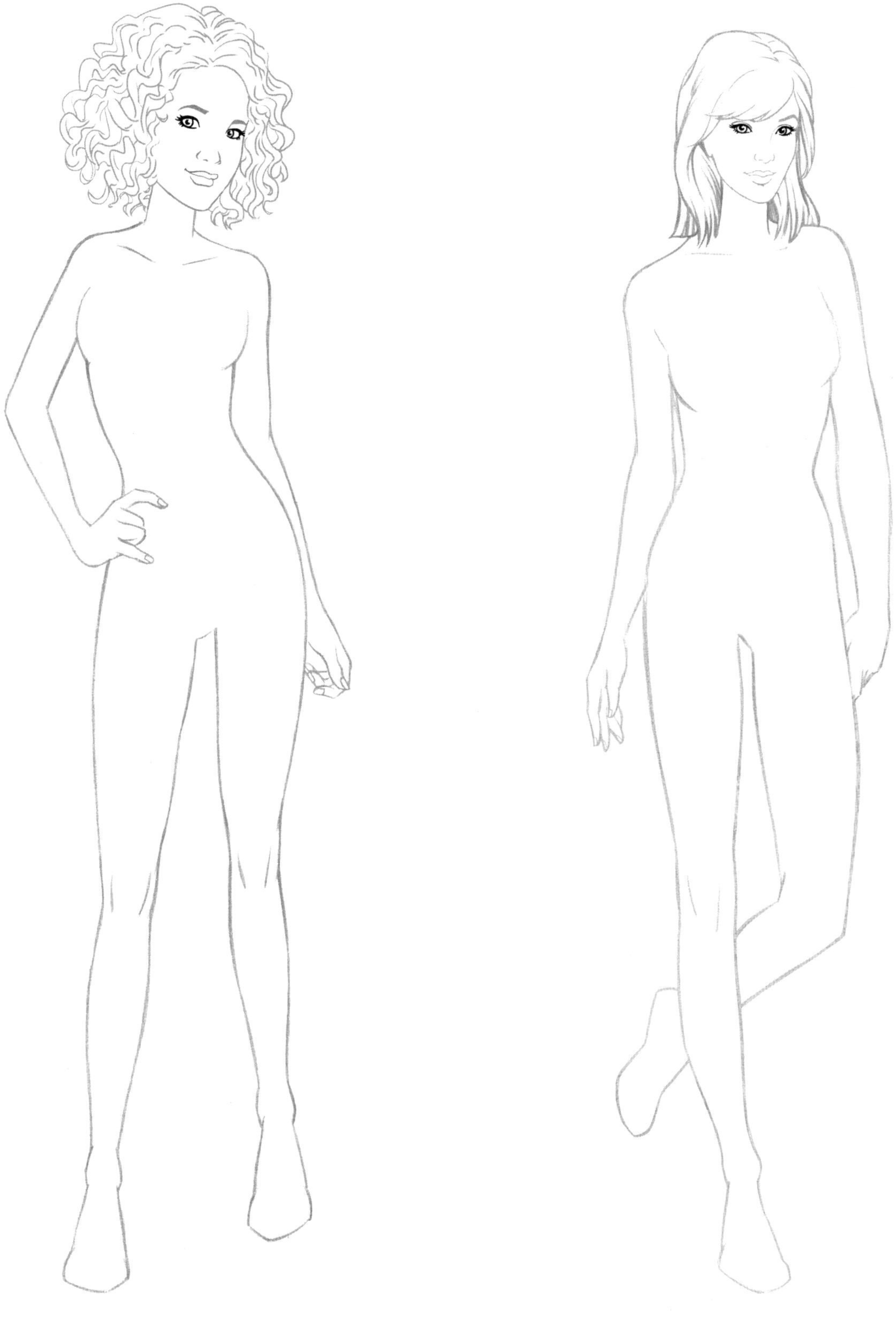

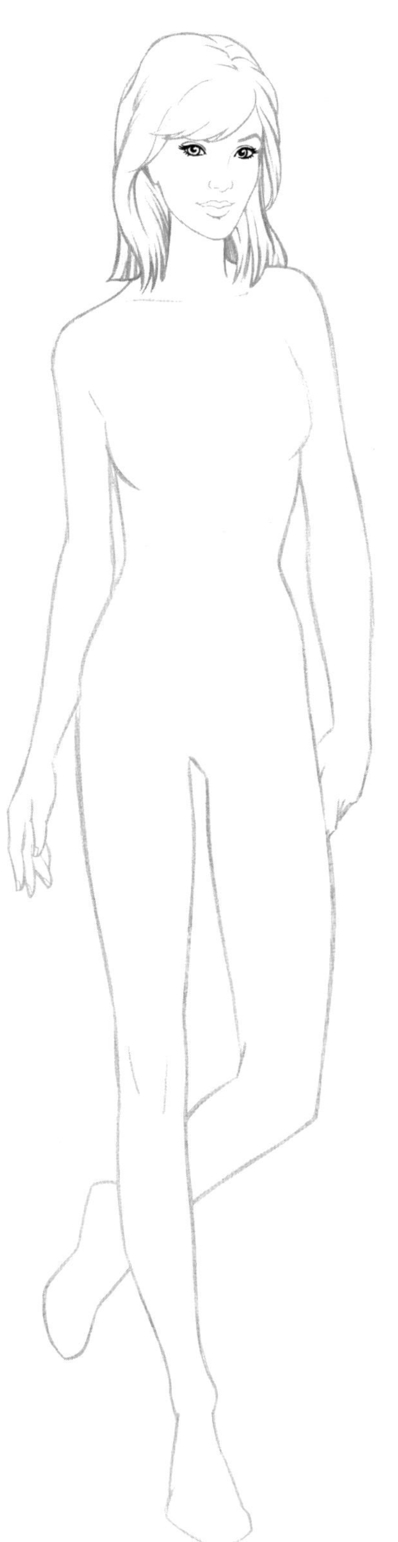

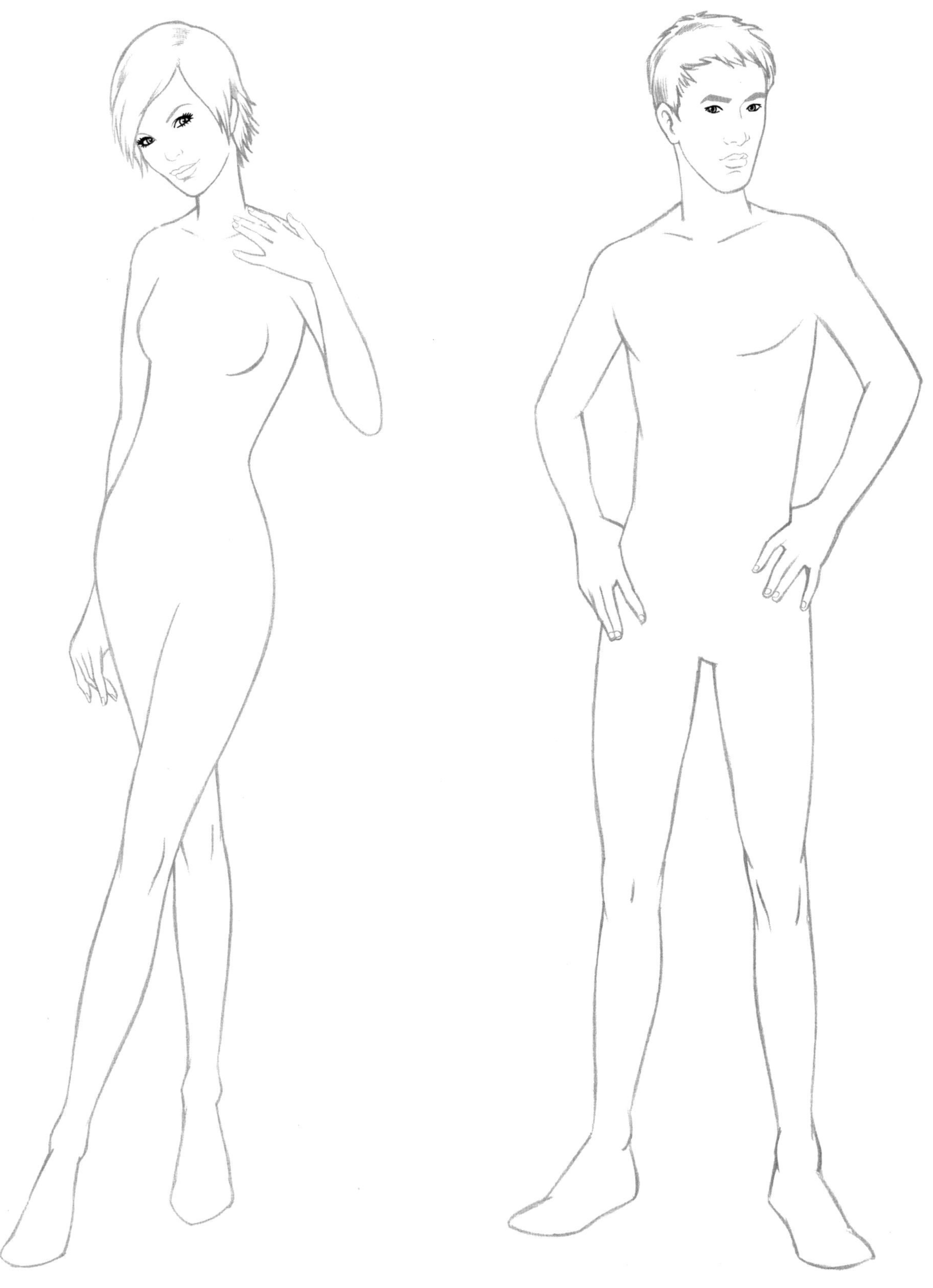

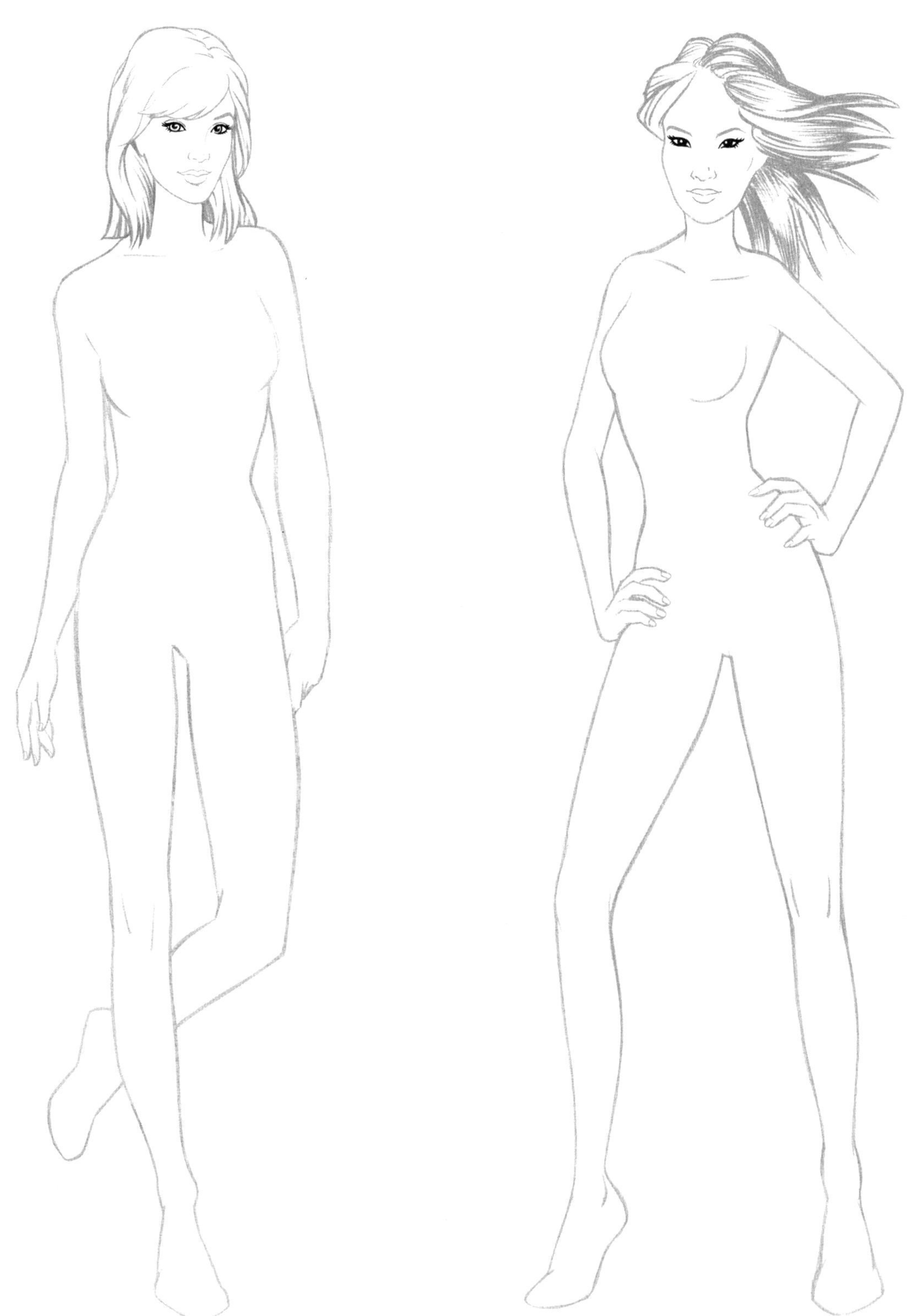

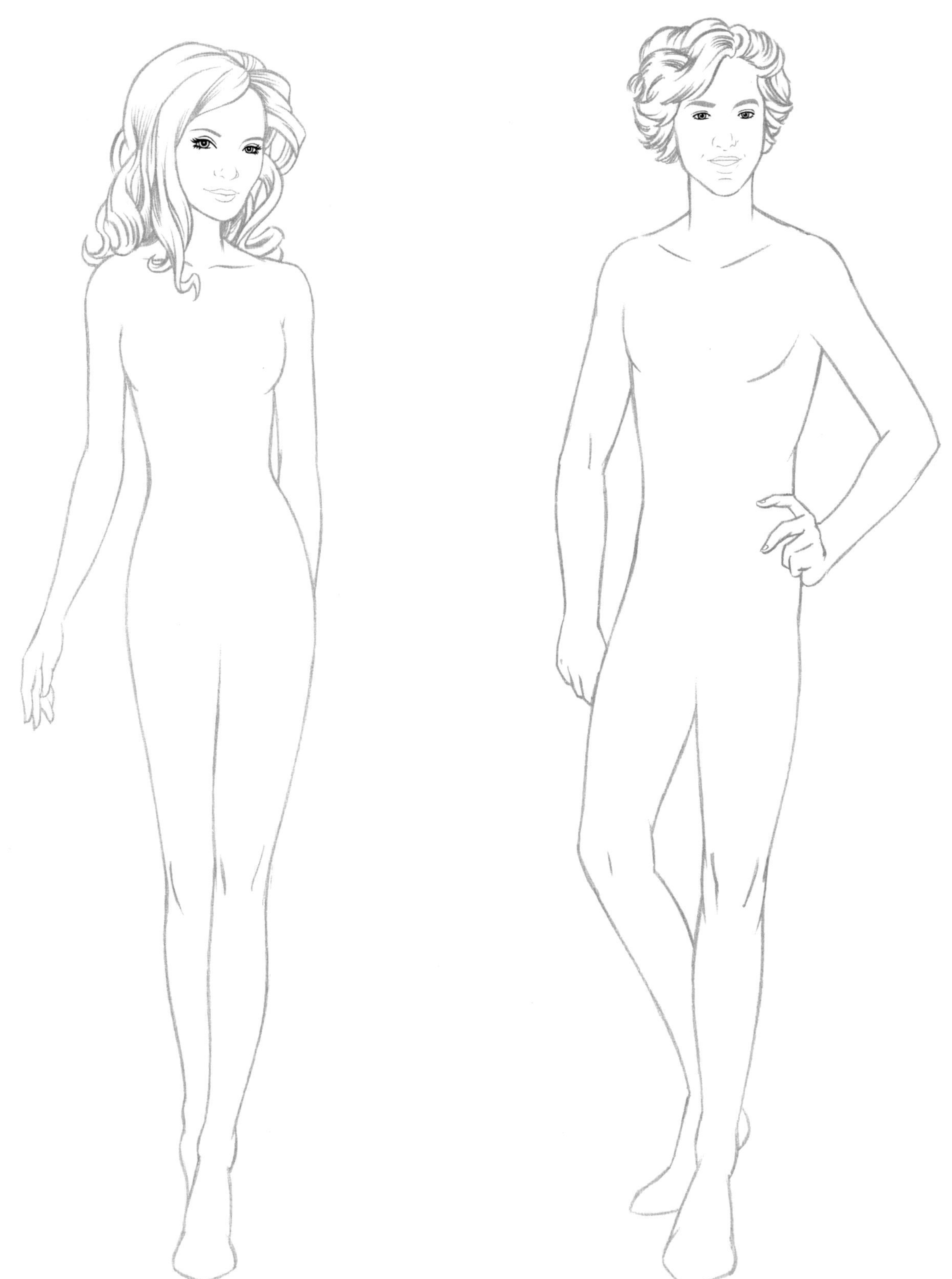

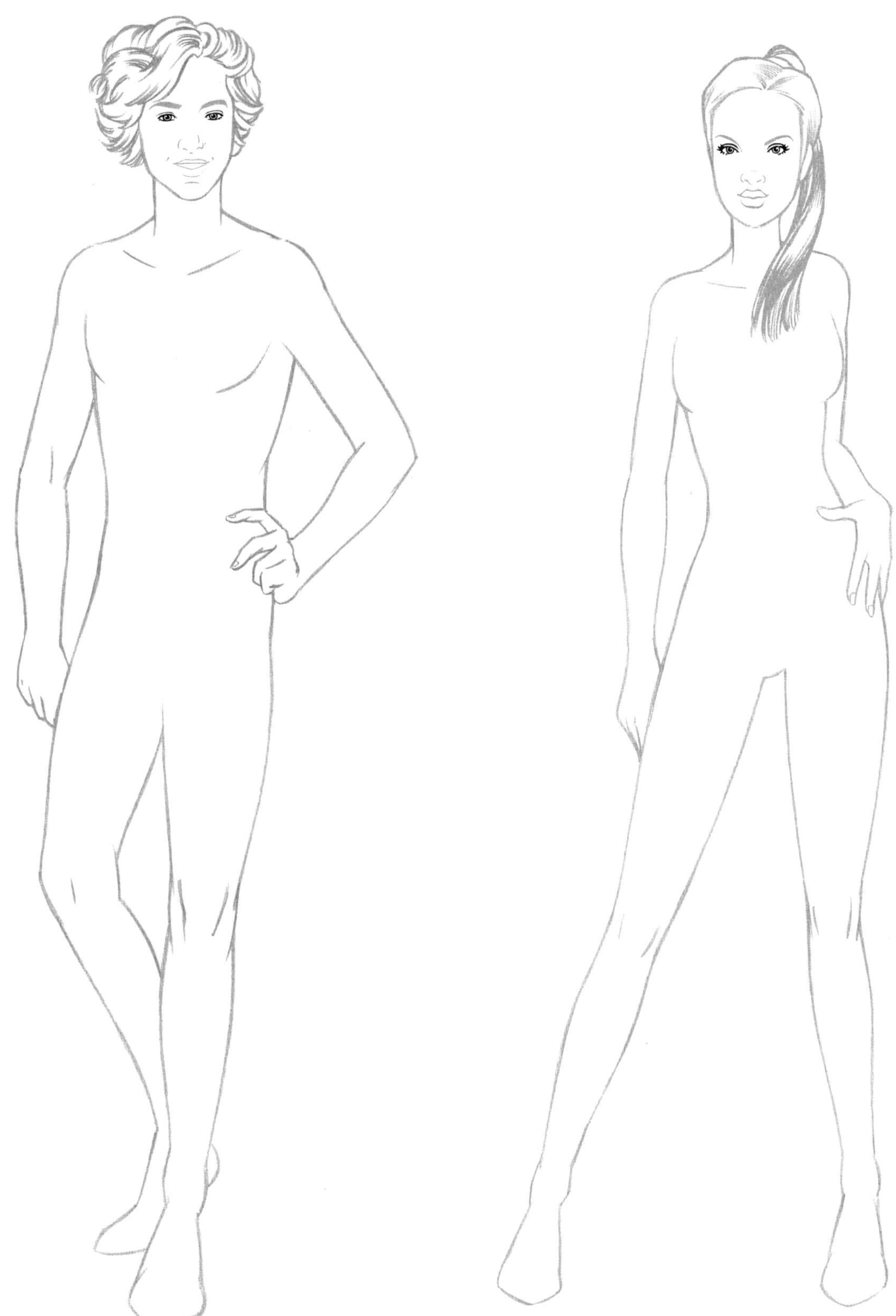

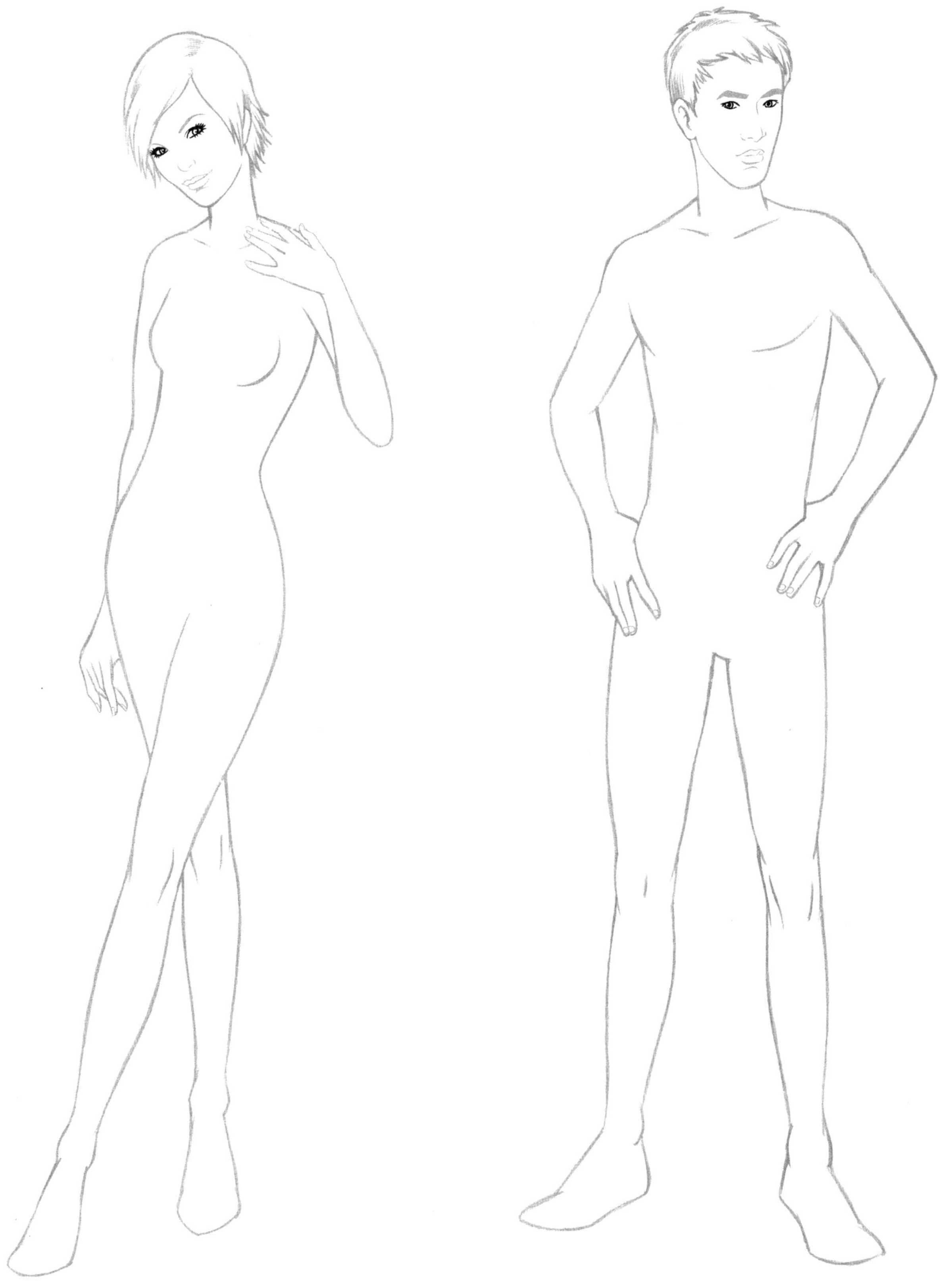

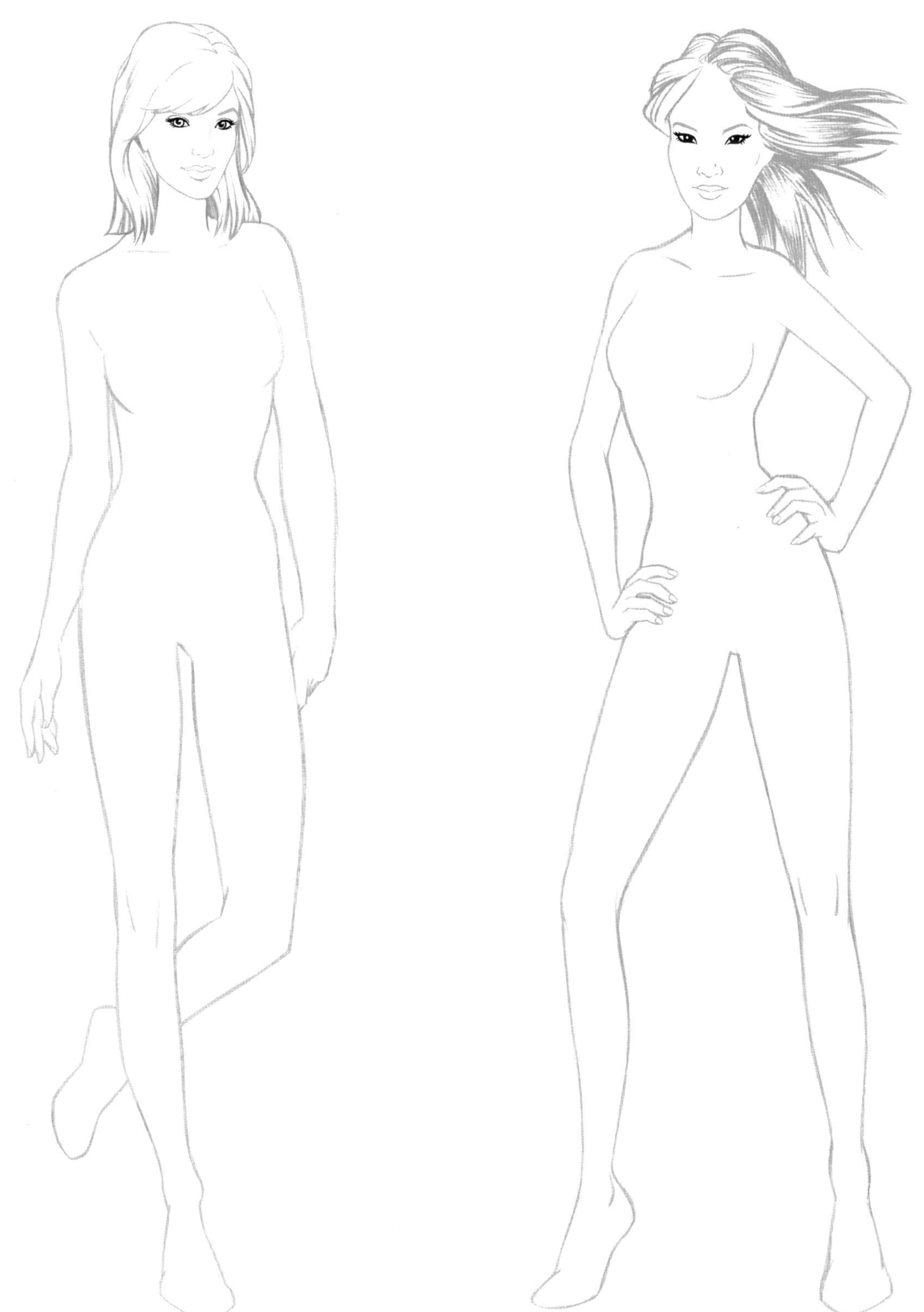

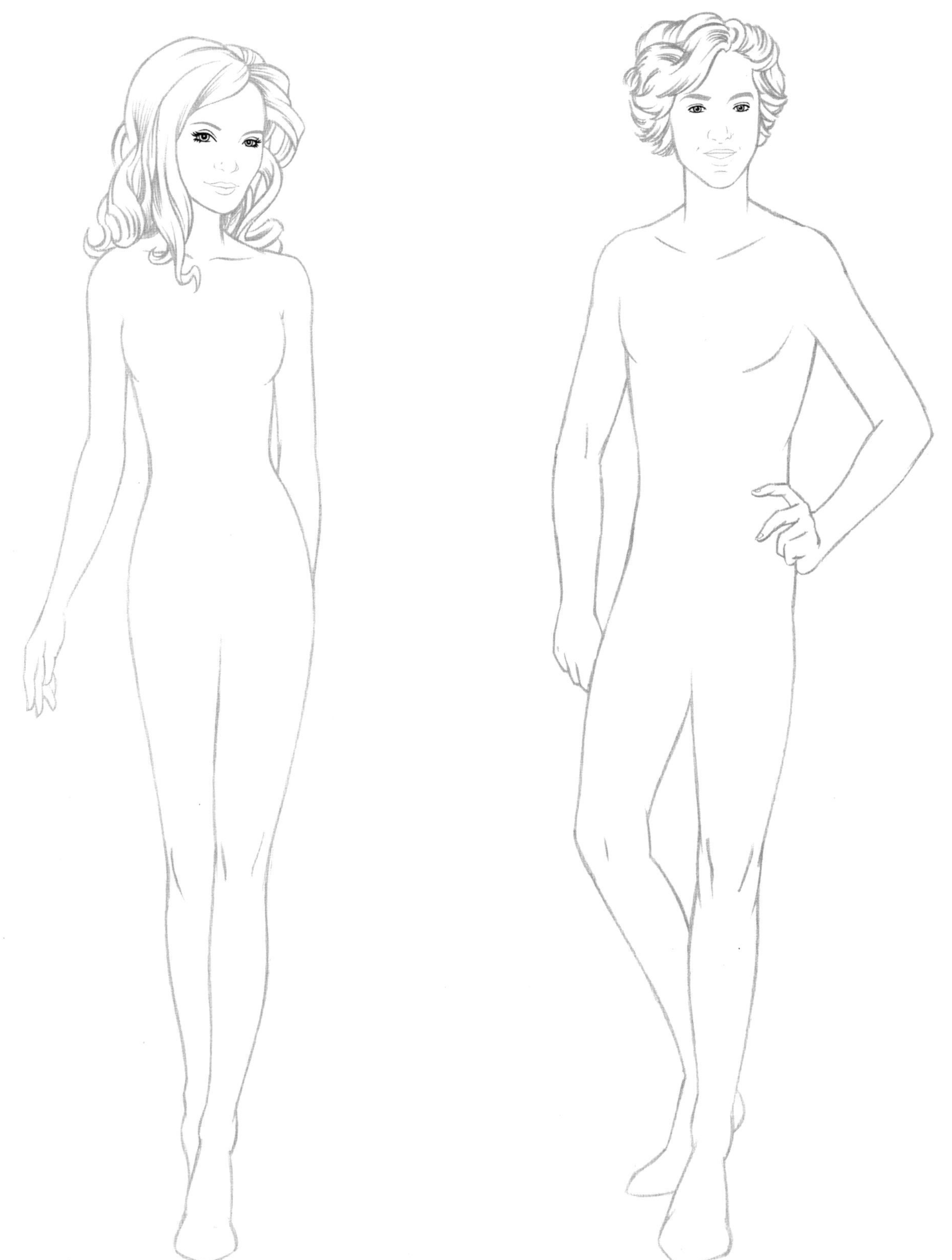

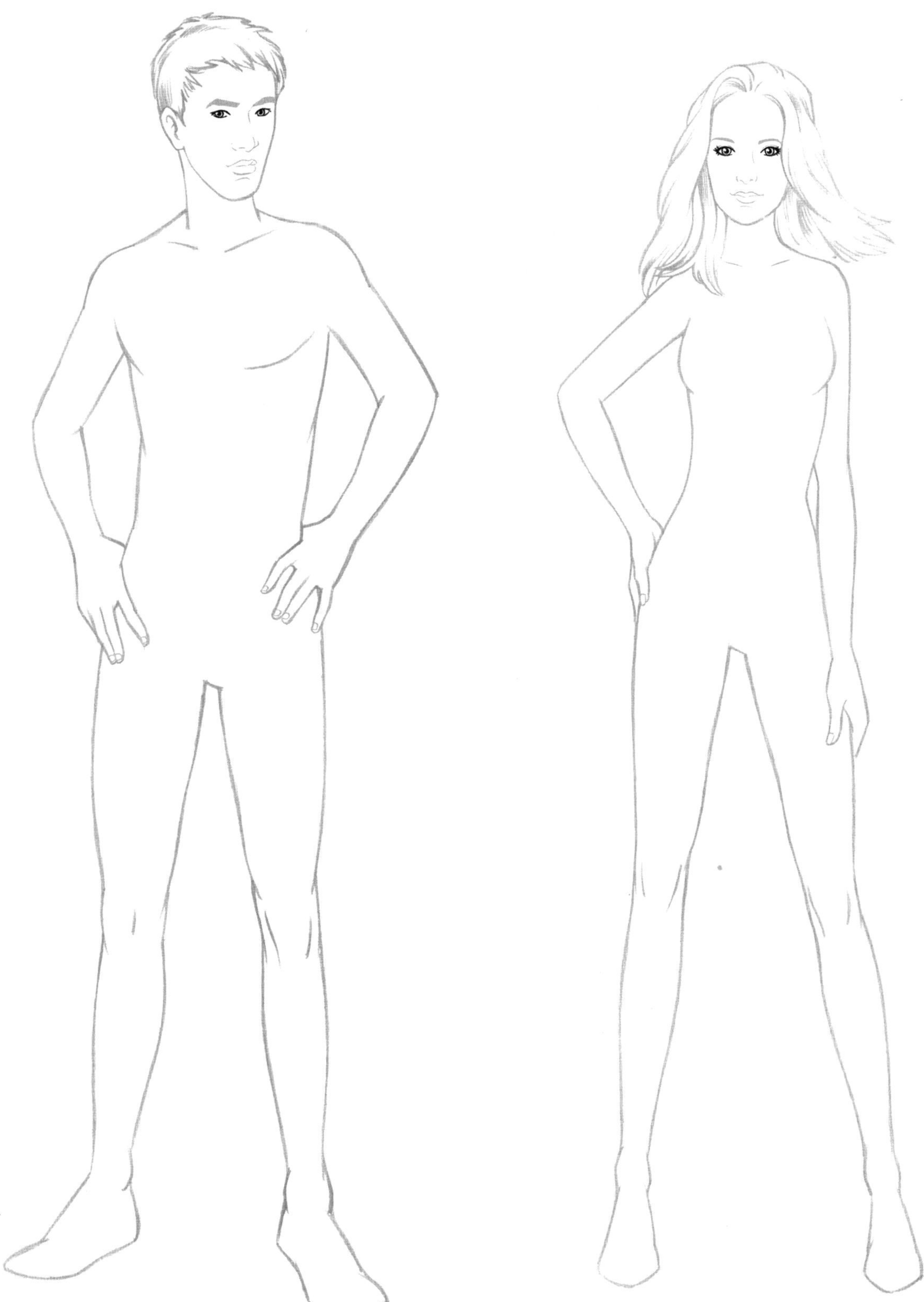

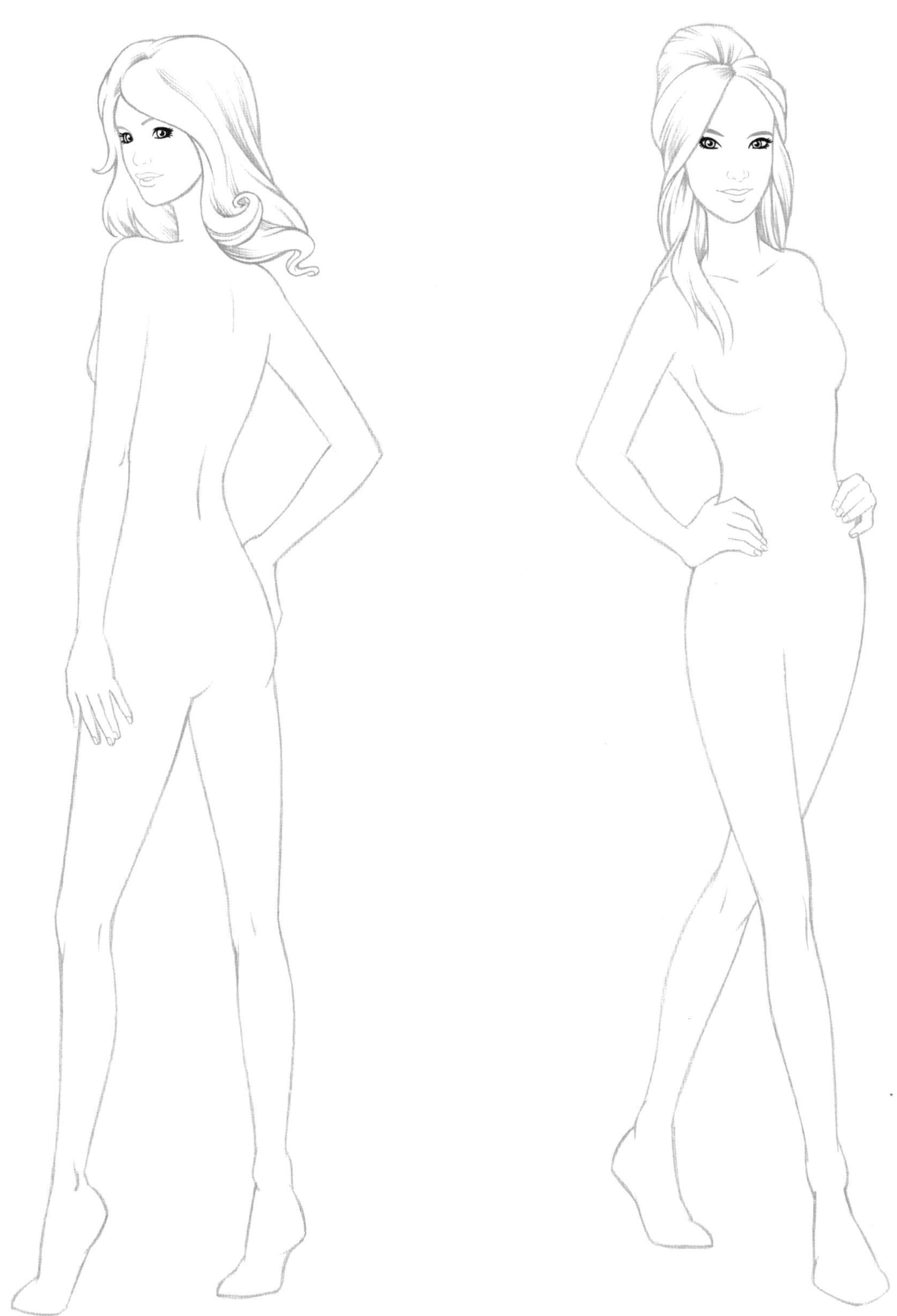

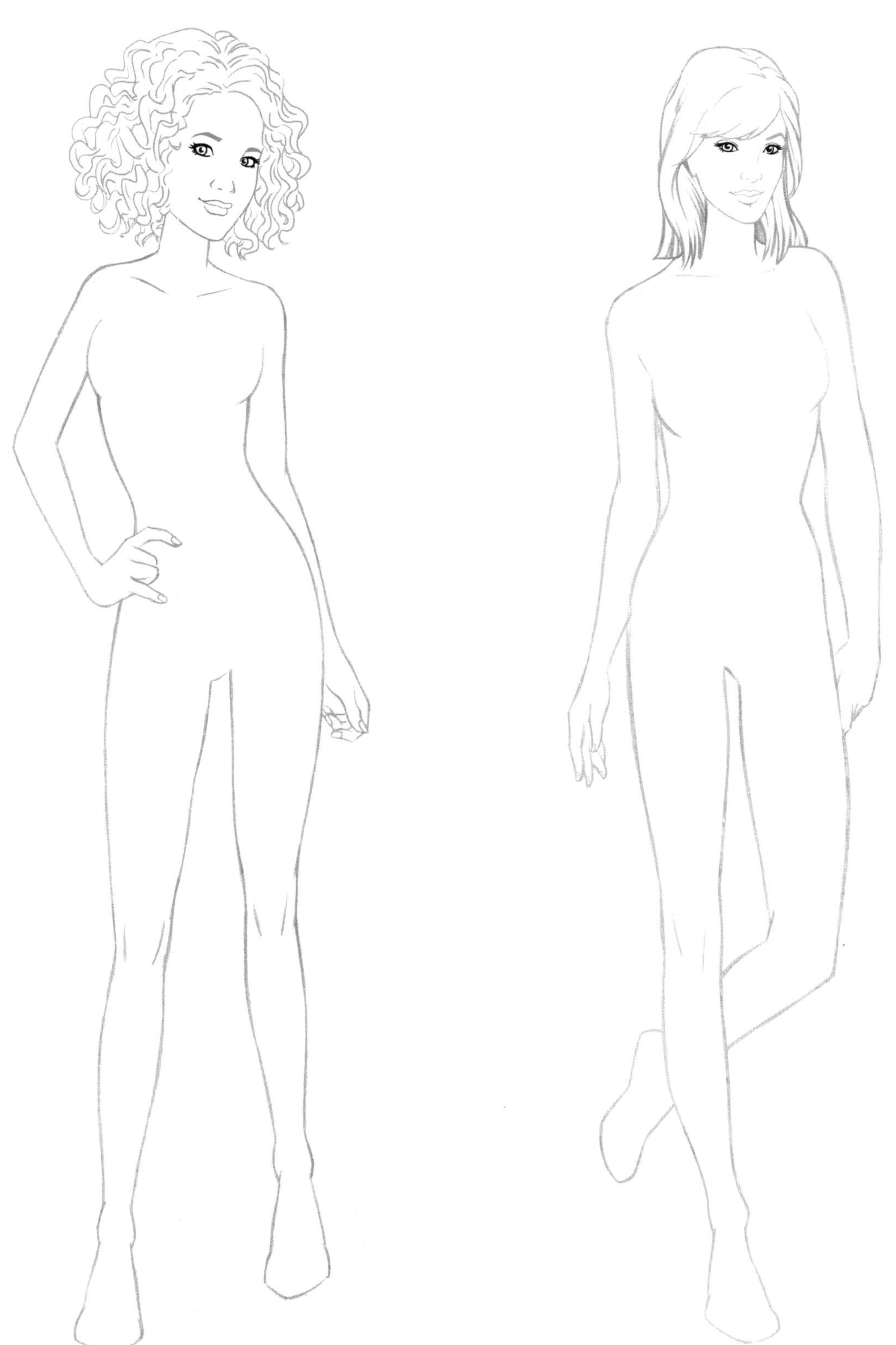

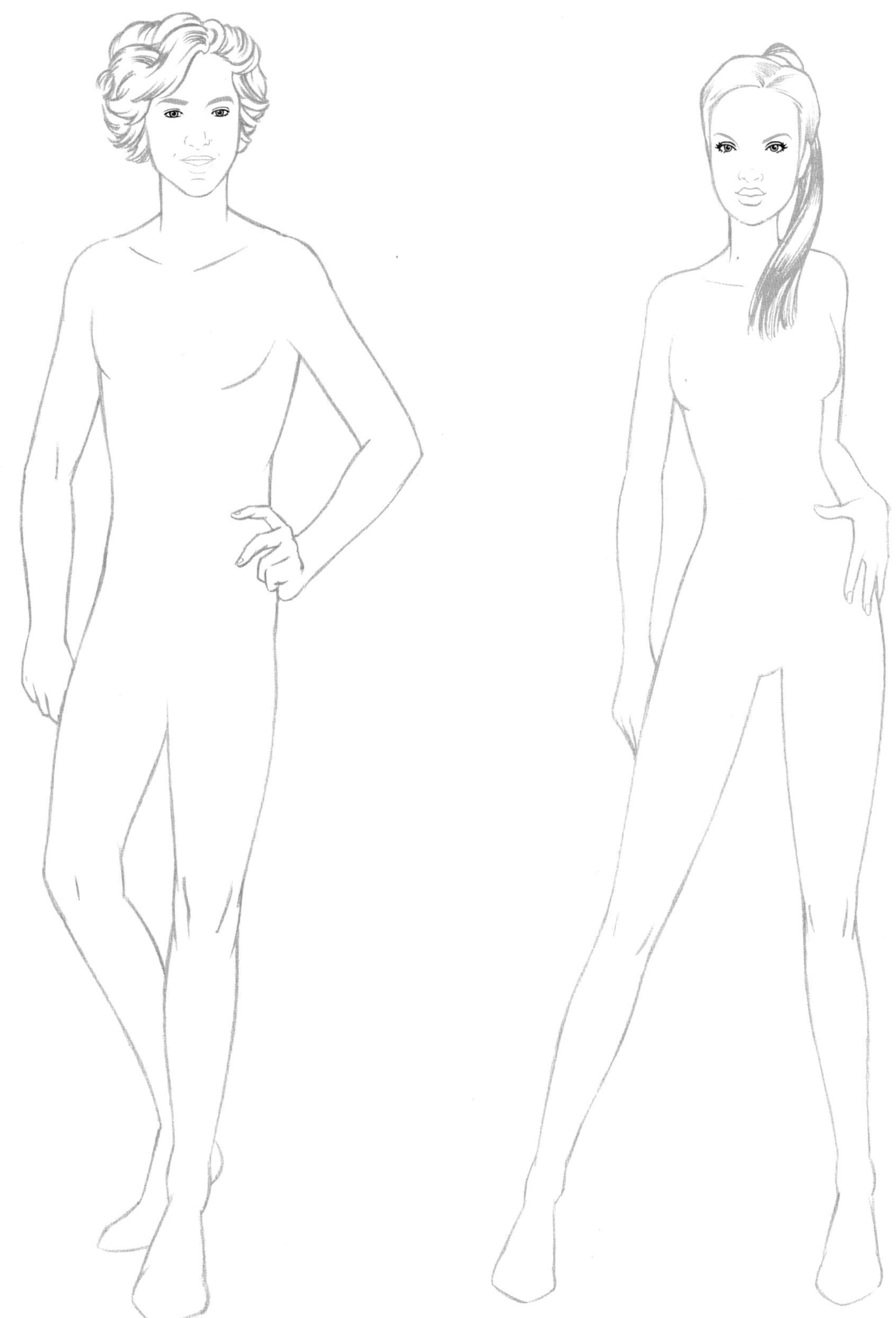